With Love for my family
You are my inspiration

Published 2013 by Lionpen Publishing, Ireland

Text & Illustration © Vincent Eke 2013

The moral rights of Vincent Eke to be identified as author and illustrator of this book have been asserted by him in accordance with the Copyright, Designs and Patents Act 1988

British Library Cataloguing Data. A CIP catalogue record for this book is available from the British Library.

ISBN 978-1-909688-00-1 Paperback
ISBN 978-1-909688-01-8 eBook-Kindle
ISBN 978-1-909688-02-5 eBook-ePub

Visit www.lionpen.com

MAMA'S TALES OF KANJI
THE TURTLE'S SHELL

By

Vincent Eke

Story Time...

It was one of those nights when up in the sky you could see the full moon, and stars hanging in divine splendour. Each star shone down upon the people below as if sending the message that their lost ones were not really gone but instead were now part of the galaxy of stars protecting them. The croaking of the frogs in the nearby pond and the chirping of the crickets in the bush beyond, exchanging pleasantries, could be clearly heard. The night air was filled with the pungent smell of burning wood. You could hear the crackling of the bamboo as it gave itself up to the overpowering heat of the fire.

Every night after their evening meal, the children of Kanji Village gathered together outside the little hut of the wise old woman. No one seemed to know her real name, if she had one. Everyone in the village simply called her Mama. The children sat on beautifully patterned hand woven mats placed on the ground to form a circle around the fire.

They listened with rapt attention as Mama told them one of her stories of their great ancestors and of the animal kingdom. Nobody seemed to know how old Mama really was. The elders in the village would tell

you that she was as old as the great Iroko tree with the big gaping hole in the trunk that stood on the edge of the forest just behind Mama's hut.

Her body was still strong and her mind still as sharp as the edge of a bamboo leaf. As Mama came out of her hut she had a welcoming smile on her face. Her all-white attire seemed to glow at the sides with shimmering brilliance. She wore a white lace blouse with small round shining plastic designs sewn into it. Tied around her waist, flowing down to her ankles, was a white wrap-around cloth. Another piece of the same material was wrapped around her upper body, going under her right armpit and over her left shoulder, as if to ward off the chill from the gently moving night wind.

Mama sat down on her special hand carved stool. It featured intricate designs of different animals such as elephants, lions, fishes, turtles, birds, antelopes and monkeys. It was said in the village that the gods had given the stool to her and that it had magical powers. It was also said that whoever sat on it would be able to understand the

language of the animals, plants and spirits. Nobody except Mama had been known to have the courage to sit on the stool.

"Mama, please tell us one of your stories about the adventures of the wise and mischievous turtle," said an excited little boy from the front row of younger children.

"Okay Cheri, I will tell you all a true story about how the turtle came to have his patched shell," Mama said with a twinkle in her eyes. "Now, my children, I want you to listen carefully and learn the wisdom of the gods from this story," she added, her voice going down a tone like the sound of the forest just before it starts to rain and all the rustling, chirping and whistling sounds suddenly cease and even the ever-hard working red ants are forced to call a break. Mama adjusted her white dress around her legs. She then looked up at the children and began her story.

A food shortage in the Animal Kingdom

Once upon a time, man and animals lived together in harmony near the Kanji Forest. The animal kingdom thrived successfully and everyone was very happy. One day the animals discovered that they were running out of food in the Kanji Forest. So the king of the animal kingdom, Lima the lion, called a meeting of all the animals to find a solution to their problem.

Lima asked Zuli the elephant to announce that all the animals were to meet at the square under the great Iroko tree by sundown the next day. Zuli the elephant climbed to the top of the highest point in the forest, Mount Kanji. At the very top he raised and stretched forward his big trunk and trumpeted the message. Even the animals at the end of the forest could hear him.

The next day at sundown all the animals were gathered as requested. Present at the square were Zingi the African fish eagle, Mani the monkey, Tobi the turtle, Padi the leopard, Jeri the giraffe, Coki the crocodile and other animals from all over the length and breadth of the forest. Lima climbed up the great Iroko tree on to the big overhanging branch.

"My fellow animals!" he rumbled. "You will have noticed that famine is creeping up on our land. We have little food left in our forest for everyone and our young ones are beginning to die from starvation."

Lima paused and looked around to assure himself that everyone was listening. "The Council of Elders has decided to seek suggestions from you all about what to do to solve our problem of food shortage until this famine wears off."

In the middle of the crowd Zingi, the fish eagle was flapping his wings.

"Yesss! Zingi, I see you want to say something. What is it you want to say?" asked Lima.

"Two days ago, in my quest for food for my family, I happened to fly past the land of the humans and I noticed that they don't look hungry," said Zingi, tucking in its wing.

"They are growing fat and I even heard the town crier announce that their king has ordered everyone to bring some of their excess food to the palace barn for storage."

"From what Zingi has seen and said, I suggest that the head of each family go to the land of the humans and get some of that food for ourselves and family," said Manki the wise monkey.

"All those in favour of going to the land of the humans to get food, indicate your approval," declared Lima.

Every animal in the square voiced their support and agreement by either raising their front paws or nodding their heads.

"Now, anyone who finds food must bring it back to this square. We will store some of the food in the great Iroko tree and the rest will be shared among every family. Anyone who disobeys or hides any food will be banished from this forest," decreed Lima the lion.

"That makes sense to me. I'm in support of that. What about you Tobi?" murmured Padi to Tobi.

"Sure, I'm okay with that," Tobi replied with a wave of his hand.

At dawn the next day some of the animals set out for the land of the humans to find food.

Tobi's secret

The next day, Tobi the turtle was walking by the edge of the forest; a hold-all slung over his left shoulder. Inside the hold-all, along with his small knife and the shovel he needed for gathering food, was a small, hour-glass shaped drum. The drum, known as a talking drum, gives out a loud melodious sound.

Tobi was singing aloud to himself when he noticed a young girl carrying a food basket filled to the brim with Chin-Chin, sweet fried chips made from bread dough. Tobi stopped and quickly hid behind a clump of bushes to watch her. She was walking alongside the forest, down the unused road which led to the king's palace. Nobody used this road anymore.

As the young girl passed Tobi's hiding place, he thought of an idea. Tobi sang his favourite song:

> *Tin tin*
> *Tinrin tin tinrin perere*
> *O pappy dey O perere*
> *O mammy dey O perere*

"I wonder where that singing is coming from," the girl said, "I know for sure that there can't be anybody around this part of the village."

The girl could not help herself, and swayed her head and hips to the sound of the song.

Tobi noticed that the young girl started to dance to his song. Then she put her basket down by the bush. He was slightly surprised by her behaviour. No human had heard his song before. Or even danced to it like this girl. Tobi stopped singing. The young girl also stopped dancing. Tobi thought of another idea. He brought out his small drum. He beat the drum once "bam!" twice "bam, bam!" and then he beat the drum repeatedly. He then started singing to his drumming. He wasn't so surprised this time when the girl started to dance once more.

As Tobi continued singing, the girl continued dancing away from her basket. The song and drumming was so melodious that the young girl danced and danced and left her food basket behind. Tobi thought

of taking the food to the square to show everybody. But on the way he changed his mind and took the food home to his family. Tobi, his wife and children were so happy that they ate all the delicious Chin-Chin.

The next day, Tobi went to the same spot again with his talking drum and waited for the young girl with the food basket to pass by. As soon as he sighted her, he began to beat his talking drum and sing the magic song. As the young girl heard the sound of the drum and Tobi's voice, she started to dance. She put down her food basket and danced more vigorously as Tobi continued singing and playing his talking drum.

After the young girl had danced away and was out of sight Tobi once again took the basket filled with Chin-Chin to his family. Then Tobi thought of a secret and easy way of getting more of the food to his house, he would dig an underground tunnel. So Tobi and his family secretly dug a curved tunnel from their house to the spot on the side of the bush path where the young girl with the food basket always passed.

On the next market day, Tobi positioned his two children at intervals inside the tunnel with his wife at the other end inside the house. Tobi then hid behind a clump of bushes close to the entrance to the tunnel opening, waiting for the young girl with the food basket to pass by again. After a short while waiting, Tobi sighted the young girl coming up the bush path. As she drew near the clump of bushes where he was hiding Tobi started to beat his talking drum.

Then he started to sing that magical song that made the young girl dance:

> *Tin tin*
> *Tinrin tin tinrin perere*
> *O pappy dey O perere*
> *O mammy dey O perere*

As the young girl heard the familiar drumming and singing, sure enough, she started dancing.

"I don't know what's happening to me," she said, her head and legs beginning to move to the music. "My head and legs just seem to have a mind of their own whenever I hear that drumming and singing."

Then she placed her food basket by the bush path so she could have more freedom to dance. As Tobi continued singing, the young girl continued dancing away from her food basket.

One of his children grabbed the food basket and emptied it into another basket which was passed on by the child in the middle of the tunnel to their mother inside the house. The girl's basket was taken and hidden away a short distance back behind some shrubs.

As soon as their mission was accomplished Tobi stopped playing his drum. The young girl also stopped dancing. She looked round but could not find her basket of food. "My basket of Chin-Chin has vanished again," she said, looking behind the shrubs and trees near the footpath where she was standing.

She kept on searching and looking everywhere but could not find her basket. Eventually she decided to give up her search. As she was walking back the same way she had come she saw the basket behind some shrubs by the footpath. It was turned upside down.

"My Chin-Chin is gone!" she said crying as she picked up her basket and found it empty. "My mother is going to be angry with me again

today. She won't believe me when I tell her what has happened."

The young girl walked back home, carrying her empty basket with tears running down her face.

"Yes, we did it!" Tobi said to his son. "Let's go home and celebrate."

They crawled back into the tunnel. Tobi covered the opening of the tunnel with dried brown banana leaves.

"I'm very proud of you, Tobi," said Mama Turtle. "You have saved our family from going hungry."

"Mama, it wasn't only Papa that did the work," said the children. "We helped as well."

"I know children," said Mama Turtle, hugging her two offspring. "I didn't forget you. Thank you Toni and Shonie for giving your father a hand to bring the food through the tunnel."

Tobi and his family had a feast that day and even had enough to keep some in storage. As time went by, Tobi and his family grew fat, robust and healthy while other animals grew thin and haggard.

Meeting at the stream

One day, as Tobi was going down to the stream he met Bongi the dog who was looking very hungry and thin, his rib cage showing through his skin.

"Greetings Bongi!" said Tobi in a singsong voice.

"Greetings to you too Tobi!" replied Bongi.

"Ahh Tobi!" exclaimed Bongi "You are looking really good. How come you and your family haven't been seen in the square since the meeting? You are growing fat and looking healthy while the rest of us are growing thin and looking sickly. Please tell me, Tobi my friend, what is your secret?"

"The secret is in the water from the stream, my friend. Drink lots of it," replied Tobi with sarcasm in his voice, as he drank water from the bank of the stream.

"That can't be your secret formula, Tobi because the rest of us also drink from this stream," retorted Bongi as he also lapped water with his tongue. "Yet we are still starving and growing thinner every day."

"Well, have it your way Bongi. I have told you my secret," said Tobi, whistling his favourite tune as he swaggered away from the bank of the stream.

"Hmm, I don't think that rascal Tobi has told me the truth. I must bring this matter to the notice of Lima the lion immediately," said Bongi, aloud to himself as he watched Tobi's back disappear into the bush.

Bongi went straight to look for Lima. He decided to run using the little strength still left in his body. He took the shortcut to the square that passes under the two arched coconut trees.

"Eh woh!" exclaimed a familiar wacky voice from the top of a nearby tree branch.

Bongi came to a screeching stop as he heard the surprised voice and looked up to find Zingi staring down at him crossly, like some hungry animal that's just missed his meal.

"Bongi! Look what you've done!" shouted Zingi, the fish eagle. "What's so important that you have to be barking and running through the woods? You just scared away the little mouse my family and I were going to have for dinner."

"I'm very sorry for scaring away your dinner Zingi, but my mission is very important," said Bongi while trying to get his breath back after screeching to a stop. "I must find and speak to Lima right away as I have news that may concern everyone in the forest."

"I'm coming with you then!" said Zingi, flying off the tree branch. Zingi flew above Bongi as he ran down the path.

Bongi and Zingi found Lima with his family at his favourite spot under the great Iroko tree. They were tossing a bone with little or no flesh on it among themselves. From a distance, both Bongi and Zingi shouted their greetings.

"Greetings to you Lima and to your family!" shouted Zingi.

"Greetings to you Lima and to your family! There is something very important that affects all of us that I must discuss with you right away," said Bongi.

"Greetings to you too Bongi, and to you Zingi!" replied Lima.

"Well! If that's the case then I invite you to come closer, Bongi my friend. There is nothing to be afraid of. My family are more scared of eating you than you are of them and as for you Zingi, by the time they'd removed your feathers from your body they would have lost their appetite," said Lima in a congenial and friendly voice.

"Thank you for your kind words Lima," said Bongi and Zingi in unison as they cautiously drew near to the lions.

"Lima, guess who I met on my way to the stream today?" asked Bongi. "I met Tobi the turtle and we went for a drink together at the stream. He was looking fat and healthy and when I asked him what his secret was he said it was from drinking lots of water from the stream," said Bongi, mimicking Tobi's voice. "But I didn't believe him. I think Tobi is hiding something very important from us."

"Mmm! You might be right Bongi. Just last night Gombi the goat told me the same thing. Unfortunately, I thought he was lying and so my family and myself had him for dinner," said Lima with just a hint of remorse in his voice. "But this time I must find out the true situation, Zingi, you go ahead, find Zuli the elephant and tell him to announce a meeting of all the animals here at the square today at sundown," said Lima.

As Zingi flew off, Lima turned to Bongi and said, "Bongi, tell everyone to be at the gathering, okay?"

"Okay Lima, see you later," said Bongi as he turned and hurriedly walked away into the bush before the hungry lions had second thoughts about not eating him.

Tobi's secret revealed

At sundown in the square under the great Iroko tree, a buzz of voices could be heard. The noise was like the sound you hear from a swarm of bees as they return to their hive with a good harvest of nectar to make honey.

Zuli the elephant blew his trunk and the clatter of voices died down until you could only hear their breathing as it merged with the sound of the forest.

Lima climbed up the great Iroko tree to the overhanging branch. He looked down at the gathering of his fellow animals and what he saw brought a lump to his throat. What used to be a gathering of happy, healthy animals was now a shambles of hungry and sickly looking animals like a dried corn cob with no corn seed.

"I have called for this gathering because news has reached me that a certain member of our community has been hiding something very important to us all," Lima the lion cleared his throat before starting

to speak again. "I have heard that Tobi the turtle and his family have found a source of food and are growing fat on it without allowing anybody else in on their secret. This behaviour is against what we all agreed on the last time we all gathered here."

"Today, Tobi is not here to tell us if this is true and so the Council of Elders and I have decided that we will send some of us to watch Tobi and his family and find out what their secret source of food is. If it is true that they have been keeping food from the rest of the community then they will be punished and the food brought to the square for everyone. All who agree say yea!" proclaimed Lima.

"Yea! Yea! Yea!" shouted the gathering of animals in unison.

"No wonder Tobi is not here this evening," whispered Agama the lizard to Hari the hare.

"I have hardly seen Mama Tobi this past couple of days at our watering hole," murmured Mama Hari to Mama Ander the antelope. And so the whispering and murmuring went round the square.

Everyone was present at the square except for Tobi and his family.

"Quiet all of you! We are sending out Bongi the dog, Zuli the elephant, Zingi the fish eagle, Ander the antelope and Hari the hare to watch Tobi and his family," said Lima in a vibrating and authoritative voice.

"And nobody is to warn them of our decision here tonight," Lima concluded.

Tobi meets an unhappy end

The next market day, Bongi, Zingi, Zuli, Ander and Hari watched Tobi and his family as they used their secret method to get food from the young girl on her way to the king's palace. Tobi and his family didn't realise that they were being watched the whole time.

The other animals patiently waited until Tobi and his family sat down to eat their meal at dinner time, then they pounced on them and arrested them.

"Greedy turtles!" barked Bongi as the other animals grabbed Tobi's wife and children.

"Selfish Tobi!" screeched Zingi.

"Tie their hands, tie the lot of them together and take all the food in the house to the square," bellowed Zuli the elephant.

"Please don't harm us!" screamed Mama Turtle and the children. "We haven't done anything wrong."

The other animal took Tobi and his family to the square where all the animals had gathered.

"Tie them up at the far end of the square," Lima said angrily. "We will all decide how to punish them after we have all eaten this food Tobi has saved."

Tobi, Mama Turtle, his son Toni and daughter Shonie were tied to trees at the end of the square. All the animals then ignored them as they went to the other side where they were all going to have a feast on the Chin-Chin and other food taken from Tobi's home.

Tobi tugged and struggled with the ropes trying to free himself. But it was no good. His ropes were tied very tight. Mama Turtle and Toni did the same but theirs were also tied very tightly.

"Mama, look, my ropes are not so tight," Shonie said. She tried moving forward and then sideways. She then pulled at her ropes. Fortunately for Shonie, her ropes got so loose that she could wriggle her way from underneath them.

Shonie hurriedly freed her father who then freed Mama Turtle and Toni. Tobi could see that the other animals' backs were turned to them as they fed on the delicious food.

"Listen, everyone. We have to run and escape from here while they are all eating," Tobi said to his family.

Tobi and his family started to creep away from the edge of the square and into the bush. As they did this they heard a shout from behind them.

"Hey! They are escaping," somebody shouted.

"Get them! Don't let them escape," they heard Lima saying.

"Run, run fast!" Tobi said to his family, "They are coming."

Tobi and his family ran as fast as they could. They did not know where they were running to. The other animals pursued them until they caught up to them at the edge of the bottomless canyon. Tobi and his family were trapped now. There was nowhere else to run. They stood and inched backwards to the edge of the canyon as the other angry animals came closer and closer to them.

"Get them!" Lima shouted. "They must be punished."

As some of the mob of animals moved forward to grab hold of them, Tobi and his family slipped at the edge and fell into the canyon.

Tobi and his family fell down the deep canyon and hit the rocks below. This caused their shells to crack in many places and they sustained several injuries to their bodies.

Luckily for Tobi and his family, they were saved from being killed by a medicine man who was out walking in the thick forest inside the canyon looking for healing plants and roots. The medicine man heard their cry for help and came to their rescue. The medicine man then took Tobi and his family home and tended to their wounds. He mixed different types of herbs together and used it to heal their bodies and glued up the shells of Tobi and his family. They stayed with the medicine man until they were well again.

After the famine was over they went back into the forest. All the other animals accepted their apology and allowed them back into the animal kingdom again.

"So my children, this is the reason why ever since the turtle's shell has had the patched shape you see today and his craftiness and wisdom has never been reduced either," proclaimed Mama as if with divine knowledge.

Around the burning wooden fire could be seen little faces, eyes and mouths wide open. Some had teardrops on their cheeks while some others had a smile on their faces and joy and laughter in their voices.

"Children, what have you learned tonight from this story?" asked Mama as she came to the end of her story.

"I have learned that being selfish and greedy is not good and could lead one to an ugly end," replied Nkechi, a beautiful young girl with plaited hair, seated in the middle row.

"I have also learned that I should honour any agreement I make with my family and friends. Therefore, I am happy that Tobi and his family got what they deserved," said another small voice belonging to Jacob, whose family lived in the next hut to Mama's.

"Once again, you have all been a wonderful audience. You have listened attentively and learned the wisdom of the gods. But above all these, children, you should learn to love and care for your community and share the resources and blessings of the land with others," concluded Mama in a loving and benevolent voice.

As the moon glowed and the stars shone ever so brightly in the late night sky, the children got up and rolled up their mats. They bade goodnight to Mama, as they walked with sleep in their eyes to their warm beds to dream of the wonderful kingdom of animals. Mama also got up and carried her stool into her hut with a happy smile on her face.

The End

Other books by the author

Look out for the next story book
from the *Mama's Tales of Kanji* series.

The Golden Bird

The Golden Bird tells the story of Tenga, a poor hunter who thinks
he can solve the famine problem in his land but ends up being
wrongly imprisoned. Tenga has to prove his innocence and goes on
to save his people from a dire famine. This friendly and easy-to-read
story teaches fair play and perseverance to today's children. It also
shows children how our everyday actions and decisions can affect
our family, friends and ultimately alter our world.

The Golden Bird by Vincent Eke

About the Author

Vincent Eke is a professional children's book writer, blogger and website developer. In addition to ***Mama's Tales of Kanji - The Turtle's Shell***, his debut early reader-grade fantasy adventure storybook, he has also written another children's picture book in this series, ***The Golden Bird*** and a new forthcoming series ***The Adventures of the Lovejoys*** for Lionpen Publishing.

Vincent Eke

Buy and download his book at these fine websites

Lionpen Publishing   http://www.lionpen.com

amazon.com Amazon   http://www.amazon.com

Smashwords   http://www.smashwords.com

Connect with Vincent Eke (Author Websites)

Lionpen   http://www.lionpen.com

Vincent Eke   http://www.vincenteke.com

Social Media Websites:

http://facebook.com/vincentieke

https://plus.google.com/110144243051754589163/

http://kred.com/ekevincent

http://ie.linkedin.com/pub/vincent-eke/59/719/67b

http://pinterest.com/vincenteke/

https://twitter.com/ekevincent

https://vimeo.com/50661684

http://www.youtube.com/watch?v=Qt0V6DP5x-E